A NOTE FF

Dear Readers:

Welcome to my "Love Unexpected" Series. For those of you who have read these books before, there is no change except for the covers. For those who are new to these books, I wrote Perfect Partners, The Right Choice, Solitary Man, and Midnight Angel early in my career. These books have been hard to find for almost a decade. Please note, no changes have been made in content from the time the books were written. As an author, I have grown and changed, but these stories hold a very special place in my heart. I'm thrilled to be able to share them with you now.

All the best,
Carly

Sign up for Carly's Newsletter:
http://www.carlyphillips.com/newsletter-sign-up/

Carly's website:
http://www.carlyphillips.com

Carly on Facebook:
http://www.facebook.com/carlyphillipsfanpage

Carly on Twitter:
http://www.twitter.com/carlyphillips

Carly on Goodreads:
https://www.goodreads.com/author/show/10000.Carly_Phillips

MIDNIGHT ANGEL

Carly Phillips

Carly Phillips

E-Book Edition CP Publishing, May 2013

New England Express

Daily Dirt Column

The pride of Acton, Massachusetts, returns! Welcome banners drape the streets of the small New England town when favorite son and Hollywood action hero comes home for Christmas. But are all residents really as thrilled as appearances imply?

Stay tuned as events unfold.

ONE

Dylan North walked down the streets of Acton, savoring the familiar sights. Old man Roscoe still sat outside the diner, refusing to give up his spot on the bench for people who were waiting to be seated. In his hometown, the cars ran at a slow pace, the people even slower. As a kid, Dylan couldn't wait to get the hell out and never look back. As an adult, he appreciated everything he'd once hated because this place possessed the peace and tranquility that were nowhere to be found in L.A.

As he strode down the street, destination in mind, one more important thought struck him, cementing his reason for coming back now. Everywhere he went reminded him of Holly Evans.

Dr. Holly Evans, he thought, shaking his head. Damn, but he was proud of her. She may not know his feelings, but by the time his short trip home was over, she'd know that and a whole lot more. But first he needed to find firm footing. To see where he stood with Holly now. They hadn't spoken in over ten years, and Dylan understood that the girl he'd left behind might want nothing to do with him. He also realized that his own feelings might have changed too. He doubted it, but he needed to keep an open mind.

He understood these things deep in his gut, in a way he couldn't have managed in his youth—and not just because his manager, his publicist and his personal assistant all told him he was an ass to turn his back on the beautiful actresses at his beck and call. Specifically Melanie Masterson, his latest and longest-lasting relationship. Melanie desperately wanted a reconciliation, but only, he thought, because being on his arm benefited her career. But he was finished hanging on to Melanie or any other woman in a futile search for the normalcy he'd experienced only once before. With Holly.

He wasn't a man prone to believing in omens, but a month ago he'd dreamed of Holly—which wasn't unusual since he dreamed of her often. But this time had been more vivid. In the dream, it was Christmas Eve and they sat in his house, opening gifts they'd bought for each other with their hard-earned money. Feeling warmer and more content than he could ever remember, he'd drowsily reached for Holly only to find Melanie in bed beside him.

The shock to his system had been greater than if he'd crawled into a cold bed all alone. It was a wake-up call he'd taken seriously.

So now he entered the office that had once belonged to Holly's father and glanced around, noting that although much was the same, such as the old doctor's diplomas and the black-and-white photos, Holly had added her own touches too. Aside from the Christmas tree in one corner, tinsel draping the walls and decals on the windows, there were more permanent fixes. She'd painted the place a cheery yellow color, a corner of the waiting room held a large toy box and a shelf filled with children's books, and an array of magazines lay on the center table.

Doc Evans had a great bedside manner, but he'd never updated the decor. His daughter had. Dylan wondered if the old man had lived to see it. Today Dylan had learned that the dad Holly adored had passed away last year, and right now her mom was out of town visiting her sick sister. Dylan hadn't been here to cushion the loss of her father. Had anyone? he wondered. The thought caused a cramping in his gut.

How many other major events had he missed in her life? And was it too late to even approach her now? So many questions.

"Can I help you?" a red-haired woman he didn't recognize asked, interrupting his thoughts as she grabbed her coat from one of the hooks in the hall.

"I'm looking for Holly—I mean Dr. Evans."

Without looking up, the other woman shrugged her coat over her shoulders. "Dr. Evans is in the back, but we've seen our last patient for the day unless it's an emergency. Is it an emergency?" As she spoke, she finally glanced into his face for the first time. "Oh my *God*! You're him! I mean, you're Dylan North. The actor."

Used to this reaction, Dylan merely treated her to his stock fan smile and reached out a hand in greeting. "Pleased to meet you."

She pumped his hand with enthusiasm until he thought his arm might fall off.

He eased his hand out of her grip. "And you are? Your name, I mean?"

"Oh, sorry," she said, her cheeks turning as red as her hair. "Nicole. Nicole Barnett. Oh my goodness, I can't believe you're standing here."

She gushed like every other fan he met, and though Dylan understood the reaction, he hoped that the more time he spent here, the more people would get used to him and treat him no differently than anyone else. Funny how after craving the spotlight, he now wanted the ordinary.

But Nicole continued to ramble in the face of idol worship. "I'd heard you were in town, and of course Holly's been talking about you, but I didn't think I'd meet you in person. Oh my gosh, this is so exciting."

"Holly's been talking about me?" His heart rate kicked up a notch. That his return was on her radar had to be a good sign.

"Your return is all anyone can talk about. Our patients keep reminding her that you two used to be an item, not that she *wants* to remember…." Nicole's voice trailed off as she realized that in her excitement, she'd slipped big-time. "I'm sorry. I really do need to get going. Should I tell Holly you're here first?"

He shook his head. "I'd rather surprise her."

Nicole grinned. "Good idea. And if you don't mind a suggestion, if she gives you a hard time, just say you're here for a flu shot. Holly can never turn down a patient in need. Unless you've already had one?" She raised an eyebrow in question.

"No, haven't had one." Nor did he desire a shot, but he supposed the cause was worthwhile. "I'll keep your idea in mind."

Nicole smiled. "It was really nice to meet you, and good luck," she told him, and eyes still impressionably wide, she slipped out the door.

Dylan exhaled hard. He hung his coat on a hook in the hall, then turned the lock, ensuring his reunion with Holly wouldn't be interrupted. In silence, he headed for the back room.

Holly stood with her back to him. Her silky blond hair had been clipped back into a ponytail that hung to her shoulders, a huge difference from the long cascading hair she had favored in high school. He couldn't wait to see it framing her beautiful face.

Since she hadn't heard his approach, he took a minute to watch. To cement his certainty that the emotions and feelings in his heart weren't shadows of the past. And doing so, he was more certain than ever that they were just as intact today as they once had been.

She scribbled in a chart and then glanced at the calendar on the wall. For a brief second, he caught a glimpse of the profile he remembered, her features more defined and grown up but still the same. Her makeup had faded from a day of hard work, something the women he knew would rarely let happen, hence the entourage of traveling makeup artists to handle touch-ups and constant trips to the restroom to powder their noses.

The woman before him was real, and he wanted her to be his again. This time forever. Steeling himself, he cleared his throat and knocked twice on the doorframe.

"I thought I told you it's okay to go home," Holly called without glancing up from replacing the paper on the examining table. "I can clean up the last few things and get the office ready for tomorrow. Go get ready for the Christmas party at Whipporwill's tonight."

Her voice hadn't changed either. The light sound was still capable of sending rippling waves of desire through him, especially when she laughed. If he accomplished nothing else on this first encounter, he wanted to make her laugh.

"It's not Nicole," Dylan said, drawing attention to himself at last.

She inhaled sharply and turned around fast. Shock, pleasure and anger all flashed across her features until finally she folded her arms across her chest, schooling her face into a blank mask. Just not soon enough to prevent him from discovering she still had a variety of feelings for him, and he hoped to tap into the more pleasant ones.

"Dylan," she said, having regained her composure.

He inclined his head. "Holly. How've you been?"

She narrowed her gaze, obviously assessing him. "Is that really the best opening line you could come up with?" she asked, then chuckled, a sound he knew was forced because it lacked the warmth and genuineness he remembered.

It didn't count as the laugh he'd promised himself. He shrugged. "I didn't think you'd appreciate it if I tossed some old line your way."

Holly nodded slowly, still unable to believe Dylan had come to see her here. She knew all about his return; how could she not when it was all her patients could talk about? But she didn't think he'd bother to look her up.

She tried to breathe steadily, a nearly impossible feat when he was still so good-looking, sexy and, damn him, charming in person. His raven hair had barely any gray and those blue eyes were just as bright.

"You're right. I wouldn't have appreciated a flip line," she said, surprised that he remembered how important honesty was to her, when he'd forgotten all about truthfulness in his rush to leave all those years ago.

She and Dylan had a history she'd never been able to forget. They'd met at thirteen when Dylan's family had moved to town, started dating at sixteen, begun sleeping together at seventeen and by eighteen and their high-school graduation, Holly had been planning their happily ever after.

She'd go to Yale University and then to medical school like her father and his father before him, and though Dylan hadn't chosen his college yet, he'd go close by, major in theater arts or drama, and they'd stick together as he tried for a career on Broadway. They'd have a house, kids and a happy life. That had been their plan, or so she'd thought until she woke up the day after graduation with a good-bye letter in her mailbox. A note on a flimsy sheet of paper, hastily written as if she'd meant nothing to him at all.

He'd been her first love, and he'd unceremoniously dumped her with the printed words *A high-school crush was never meant to last. It's time we both move on. Dylan.* Not even *Love, Dylan.*

Then he'd gone on to change his name from Dylan Northwood to Dylan North and quickly became America's heartthrob, staring at her from the cover of every magazine in the supermarket and drugstore.

Now he stood before her. Holly exhaled slowly, trying not to let Dylan see that his return had her trembling.

He stared with the half smile and the dimple America adored on his face. "How about a hello hug for an old friend?" he asked with more than a hint of challenge in his voice.

Touching him would be like looking for an electric shock, but if she turned him down, he'd assume she still had feelings for him. Which she didn't, she assured herself. None at all.

Liar. "Yeah, I think I could manage a hug. For a friend," she added, more for her benefit than his.

She stepped forward and was immediately surrounded by his heady masculine scent and engulfed by his strong arms and a wealth of emotion she'd tried hard to bury. Her cheek nestled into the nubby wool of his sweater, and his jean-clad thighs brushed against her light slacks.

Shaking, she stepped back before she embarrassed herself, the practiced smile she reserved for her most trying patients on her face. "So what brings you by?"

His steady gaze met hers. "I couldn't come home without seeing my Midnight Angel… I mean, without seeing you again."

She swallowed hard, his use of the endearment taking her off guard. Dylan's father had walked out when he and his sister were young, only to return again for another try. When that second chance failed a few weeks before Christmas their junior year in high school, his mother had broken the star on their Christmas tree in frustration. Holly had bought the family an angel to put on top instead. New memories to replace the old, she'd explained when she'd given it to him at midnight on Christmas Eve.

He'd called her his Midnight Angel.

She'd believed they would last forever.

She shivered and forced herself back to the present. "Well, I'm glad you came by. It was good to see you again." And it would be just as good to have him gone. "As you can see, I was just finishing up here. I've had a long day."

She was sure she looked as exhausted as she felt, yet somehow she resisted the urge to fix her hair or excuse herself and run to her office to touchup her makeup. This was who she was. No sense hiding it. Though she considered herself attractive on a good day, today wasn't one of those.

The Hollywood hunk might have dated her once, but the gorgeous women he saw daily and at award shows and premieres made her look like roadkill in comparison. Especially in contrast with Melanie Masterson, the actress the magazines constantly paired him with.

He glanced at his watch. "Actually, I was hoping you had time for one more patient today."

"You?" she asked, surprised. He didn't look sick.

"Flu shot. I never managed to get one before I left L.A." He shoved his hands into his back pockets and grinned at her like an adorable little boy who'd forgotten his lunch money and was begging for a loan.

The effect was potent, more than any other good-looking man had had on her ever. Guiltily, thoughts of John, her on-again, off-again boyfriend, arose. She and John had started dating when she'd returned home to take over her sick father's practice a little over a year ago. But while John was ready to settle down and had begun pressuring her for more of a commitment, she wasn't ready, and lately she'd been wondering if she ever would be.

She'd been putting him off with flimsy excuses, but *I need more time* and *Let's get to know each other better* didn't hold much weight when they'd known one another since grade school. John provided comfort and ease but not this overwhelming sexual desire she felt just looking at Dylan again.

"Hello?" Dylan waved a hand in front of her face. "I asked if you'd give me a flu shot." He studied her with concern.

She shook her head to clear her thoughts and focus on keeping Dylan in the past where he belonged. Forcing a smile, she said, "Sure. I can manage one more shot."

She gave him a quick exam, not wanting to spend too much time examining his broad, tanned, muscular chest or any other part of his body that created that longing feeling swirling inside her. After a quick escape to gather her equipment, she walked back into the exam room.

"So are you going to Whipporwill's tonight?" he asked about the town's annual Christmas party. He pushed up his sweater sleeve in preparation for his shot.

She shook her head. "I haven't had any down-time lately. I thought I'd head home and relax." In fact, she'd already called John and cancelled, claiming exhaustion. Her bed beckoned.

Once she'd slept, she would wake up refreshed and full of holiday spirit, ready to shop for the gifts she normally purchased way ahead of time. But since her father died, she'd been so busy keeping his practice alive that she'd had no time for anything that resembled fun.

"That's too bad. I was hoping I could steal a dance."

She shot him a disbelieving glance. A dance? Was that something like their hug? Did he really find being around her that easy, making conversation that simple, as if they'd never meant anything to each other beyond friends? Was the attraction that swirled inside her even now nonexistent for him when he looked at her? She clenched her jaw in pain and frustration.

"I thought we could hang out and catch up. You know, like old times. Come on, Holly. Please?"

She closed her eyes and counted to ten, seeing her relaxing night evaporate. If she didn't show up at the party, Dylan would think she was avoiding him, or worse, running from her feelings.

"Fine," she said with forced cheer. "I'd love to hang out with an old *friend*." As long as he didn't call her his Midnight Angel again.

And since he found it so easy to be her *friend*, she decided there was a nice, fleshier place than his arm for her to insert the needle for his shot. One where he wouldn't forget her quite so easily this time.

"Oh, Dylan? I need you to do me a favor first."

He grinned, obviously pleased she'd agreed. "What's that?"

"Drop your pants."

He groaned, and she laughed, her first free and easy laugh since he'd walked into her office unannounced.

TWO

Whipporwill's was the fanciest restaurant in Acton and often doubled as a catering hall for weddings and other assorted affairs. By L.A. standards, it fell short of chic, and by Boston standards it was a family-style restaurant at best. Still, it was the best Acton had to offer, and tradition dictated the whole town show up for an annual bash the week before Christmas.

Dylan leaned against a scarred, wood-paneled wall, smiling and greeting friends, both old and new. His mother, Kate, stood on the opposite side of the room, holding court, gesturing proudly to her famous son. He'd flown his mother to L.A. a few times a year and he'd come home to visit and left just as quietly. Having him here to show off was a first, and she reveled in the attention. Meanwhile, he was looking around for Holly, who was nowhere to be found.

Dylan had all but dared her to show up tonight. In his arrogance, he'd thought that just because he'd once been able to anticipate her actions, he could still do the same. But as the minutes passed, he was forced to admit he'd miscalculated. Badly enough for him to admit defeat.

Before he could come up with an excuse that his mother and everyone else would accept so that he could leave gracefully, a guy he recognized from high school walked over and joined him.

"Dylan, I heard you were in town. It's good to see you." The other man held out his hand.

Dylan grinned. "John Whittaker? Damn, it's been a long time." He pumped his old friend's hand.

"Last time I saw you, we were cleaning toilet paper off the football field to keep Coach from calling the cops and reporting the school had been vandalized."

Dylan laughed. "I remember." It had been their high-school graduation farewell prank. Dylan had left for L.A. a few days later.

"I can't tell you how many times I've thought of that night over the years. Every time I see your ugly mug on the cover of a magazine, in fact." John shoved his hand into the back pocket of his chinos.

He still favored the preppy look while Dylan had always liked jeans and T-shirts best. Unlike many of the guys Dylan had greeted tonight who sported bald spots or comb-overs, John still had a full head of sandy-brown hair.

"Tonight must feel like a high-school reunion for you," John said, understanding in a way that surprised Dylan.

He grimaced. "Worse. I think you're one of the first people who's happy to see me for the right reasons." *Friendship, not awe*, he thought.

"As soon as they all realize you're still the same, the fame thing'll pass."

Dylan shrugged. "I hope you're right. So what've you been up to?"

"I work at an investment firm in downtown Boston," John said, propping one shoulder against the wall.

"That suits you. Married?"

"Not yet, but I'm trying to get the woman I've been seeing to settle down."

"Anyone I know?" Dylan asked.

John studied Dylan in pointed silence. "Actually—" John's cell phone rang, cutting him off. He glanced at the incoming number. "Hang on, and we'll pick this up in a few minutes," he said to Dylan. He answered the call, walking off to talk in private, leaving Dylan to watch the door some more and hope Holly would show up after all.

* * *

After heading home for a nap, a shower and some serious primping, Holly met up with Nicole on the steps outside Whipporwill's. The chill in the air and impending snow signaled Christmas was coming soon. Holly loved the holiday season. She was suddenly glad she'd come tonight, and the festivities weren't the only reason. Neither was the challenge Dylan had issued earlier. Dylan himself was the man motivating her actions.

"I still think you should have surprised John instead of calling him and telling him you'd decided to come tonight," Nicole said, interrupting Holly's thoughts. "Spontaneity is good for relationships, and from what you've told me, John could use some good old-fashioned surprises in his life."

Holly couldn't deny that comment. "I just thought he deserved to know I'd changed my mind." She'd show up at the party, spend time with both the past and present men in her life and hopefully leave Whipporwill's with a clear mind, ready to move on.

"I bet you were afraid he'd think you came just to see Dylan," Nicole said knowingly.

With a groan, Holly pulled open the door and entered the festive party. Red and silver velvet bows adorned the walls, and tinsel fell enticingly from each potted plant and fern, while poinsettias were strategically placed around the room, their beauty enhancing the holiday atmosphere.

"Do you want to stick with me?" she asked Nicole, knowing her friend was still fairly new to town and didn't know everyone yet.

Nicole shook her head. "Actually, I see someone I want to talk to," she said and, with a brief wave, disappeared into the crowd.

So much for needing a guiding hand, Holly thought wryly. She paused to hand her jacket to the coatcheck girl before heading inside.

No sooner had she glanced around than her first challenge came to greet her. "Holly, I'm so glad you changed your mind and decided to come," John said, grasping her hand in his. "You look beautiful."

"Thank you." She took in his polished look, the pressed chinos and collared shirt paired with a polo sweater, and smiled. "You look pretty good yourself." She kissed his clean-shaven cheek, his familiar aftershave surrounding her.

"Well, well, look who decided to show up after all."

Dylan's deep voice sent sizzling awareness shooting through her veins, leaving no part of her body unaffected. While John's scent had been warm, *Dylan's* cologne caused a distinct path of heat to travel along her nerve endings and settle in the pit of her stomach.

"I thought you said you'd be missing this shindig." He cocked his head and pinned her with a knowing grin.

"You two have seen each other already?" John asked, obviously surprised.

Dylan was the one subject John never broached with Holly. He knew the history. He'd been through school along with them, but John and Holly had begun dating once they'd returned home as adults. As if by mutual agreement, they'd left Dylan behind and started fresh. But Holly realized that

Dylan had always been with her even when she wasn't aware of it.

She wondered if Dylan had heard she and John were an item. She wondered if he'd even care. After clearing her throat, she tackled John's comment. "Dylan stopped by the office this afternoon."

"I wanted her to promise me a dance tonight," Dylan said with that sexy look back in his gaze.

Obviously he hadn't heard anything about her and John being a couple. She winced and jumped to explain his comment to John. "Actually, Dylan came by for a flu shot."

She didn't want John to get the wrong idea. *Or was it the right one?* Holly wondered, her traitorous heart beating hard in her chest because Dylan was near. Obviously the old feelings weren't gone. Not even the anger or sense of betrayal, which still lay in her heart like lead, could dilute the spike of desire he caused.

"The good doctor didn't mind giving me one, either." Dylan grinned and rubbed the affected spot just below his hip. He laughed until his gaze fell to Holly's hand, still enclosed in John's grasp.

His eyes opened wide, and an uncomfortable silence fell until finally Dylan spoke. "This is the woman you've been seeing? The one you've been trying to get to settle down?" His voice sounded hoarse to Holly's ears as he cocked his head to one side, understanding dawning.

Instinct had her pulling her hand back from John's.

"And you're the reason she's been avoiding commitment. I don't know why I didn't realize it before," John said, sounding certain of his conclusion.

"Excuse me." Holly interrupted the two men. "But could you both stop speaking about me like I'm not here?" She turned to John first. "Dylan has nothing to do with my feelings about commitment," she assured him. But her queasy stomach and sweaty palms made her wonder if her words were a lie.

"I know you want to believe that, but I'm ready to move forward with you or without you." John turned to Dylan. "How long are you in town for?"

Dylan looked as stunned as she felt as he replied, "Through Christmas, but—"

"That's decided, then."

"What is?" Holly asked, nothing around her making sense.

John stood up straight and pulled his coat check ticket from his pocket. "Spend the next few days with Dylan or alone with your own thoughts—I don't care which. But deal with the past and decide what you want for your future."

Holly blinked. "Can someone please tell me when I lost control of my life?"

"Oh, about the time this guy took off for Hollywood." John reached out and squeezed her hand tight. "I care about you, and I want what makes you happy. But I want to be happy too, so let's both agree to use these few days wisely, okay?"

She had thought she would walk in here tonight, take one look at John, who was ready to give her a future, take one look at Dylan, who'd caused her nothing but pain, and be ready to ride off into the sunset with John. Well, her thinking had been naive in the extreme, because Dylan wreaked a kind of havoc on her body and soul that she couldn't explain or understand. He promised nothing, and yet she couldn't give herself completely to any other man.

She had to take this time with him now. Knowing John had understood that even before she had, she nodded. "Okay."

To her shock, John turned and shook Dylan's hand, then kissed Holly on the cheek, not on the lips. Not, she noticed, like a man staking his claim or giving her something to remember him by as she weighed her options. But, then, she and John had always been about companionship and caring, not all-consuming love and desire. Wasn't that what made him the perfect choice for her future?

Dylan's return was temporary, and he certainly wasn't offering forever. They barely knew each other anymore. Yet she felt like she still did know him. So even if the likelihood was that he'd leave for L.A. and her heart would be broken once more, she needed closure. Once again something John had understood before she had.

"Well, well, that certainly was interesting." Dylan watched John's retreating back. "I had no idea you two were involved."

His voice brought Holly back to the present. To the man who'd caused more upheaval in her life than anyone she'd ever known. "How would you know anything about me? It's not like you kept in touch over the past decade."

"True." He inclined his head. "And I'm sorry for that. I'm sorry for a lot of things we've yet to hash out. But I'm back now and plan to make up for lost time." His eyes glittered with determined fire.

The same fire she'd bet kept him stoked and primed as he'd quickly climbed through the ranks in Hollywood. Holly shivered. "What makes you think I want the same thing?"

He shook his head and let out a low, chiding sound, but his lips were turned upward in a grin. "Don't make me kiss you senseless in front of this crowd just to prove a point." He leaned in closer, his roughened cheek against hers, making her skin tingle. "Because when I kiss you again, and you can be sure I will, we're going to be alone, where I can take my time and go oh so slow and deep." His husky voice rumbled over the last two words.

Her breath caught in her throat, and her own vivid imagination took over. She envisioned his lips covering hers, his tongue thrusting inside her open mouth while his body made love to hers just as he'd described.

A low moan escaped her throat, but thank goodness the music was loud and their audience, though rapt, couldn't possibly capture the subtle undercurrents running between them.

"Don't you have a beautiful girlfriend waiting for you in LA.?" she asked, wondering why he was bothering with seductive come-ons with *her*.

"Nope." His serious blue-eyed gaze met hers.

"The papers said—"

"The first thing you're going to need to learn is that you should never ever believe anything you read in the papers, respectable publication or otherwise. Always confirm the story with me first, or better yet, trust your gut."

"You talk like you're going to be around long enough for it to matter. It doesn't. I'm sorry I even brought up the subject."

"No you aren't, and neither am I. I want you to know everything about me now, just like I intend to learn everything about you. But first, I want that dance you promised me."

"I never—"

His finger halted her moving lips, the touch both firm and gentle. "Are you going to deny us something we both want?"

She sighed, then placed her hand in his and let him wind their way to the dance floor. His hand came to rest at her waist, intimately pulling her against him until their lower bodies swayed in unison to the sultry beat of the music.

She shut her eyes and gave herself over to feeling, suddenly understanding why John had never been enough. Why no man had ever come close. No one could ever live up to the memory of her first love, and now he was back, wreaking havoc with her life again.

Though she was older and wiser this time, the thought gave her no sense of comfort because she was no more in control of her emotions and desires than she was over the inevitable outcome of this brief reunion.

* * *

The snow had started falling sometime during the party. White flakes drifted down and stuck to the ground and, combined with the weather forecast over the next few days, brought with them the certainty of a white Christmas. It'd been years since Dylan had enjoyed snow and even longer since the promise of tomorrow looked so damn good.

He waited as Holly pulled her wool coat tight around her and cinched the belt at her waist. Dancing with her, holding her in his arms again, had convinced him this return home had been exactly what he needed. And if the byplay between Holly and John was any indication, Dylan was exactly what she needed too. He hated like hell that his old friend John would be a casualty, but obviously things between him and Holly hadn't been all that good before Dylan returned to the picture.

Dylan knew Holly was wary and had good reason to mistrust both him and his motives, but he'd made progress already. He had but one crucial week to cement her trust.

"Ready?" he asked her.

She nodded.

"Where do you live now?"

She pulled on a pair of black gloves. "I took over the apartment above the office that Dad used to rent out to students."

"Smart move. So you walked here?"

"Yes." She inclined her head. "What about you? Are you staying with your mother?"

"Would she let me live if I didn't?" He chuckled. "She's so happy to have me back home that she's already cooked me breakfast, lunch and dinner."

They started down the street.

"Careful or she'll spoil you. Do you cook for yourself back home?"

He took the fact that she was asking questions about his life as a positive sign. "If it can be defrosted in a microwave and zapped, I can cook it," he said proudly.

She laughed, and the sound carried on the wind, churning in his gut. "That sounds pretty close to my life lately. But I hired a partner who's supposed to start working after the first of the year, and I really hope it'll take some of the burden off me!"

"Assuming the old folks take to her?" Dylan asked knowingly.

"It's a him," Holly said. "Lance Tollgate. I think the patients will like him," she said, her voice warming. "He's young and friendly, and he's got kids, so he can relate to the grandparents and parents. It should be a good fit."

"Your father would be really proud of you."

"Yeah, he was." Her voice cracked with emotion. "Sorry. It just hasn't been that long."

Dylan swallowed hard. "I'm sorry I wasn't here." He reached for her hand and held on tight.

"I got through it. There was a lot you weren't here for," she reminded him.

He knew they'd have to discuss and deal with his abrupt departure if he had any hope of her believing he wouldn't abandon her again. But he wanted her to get to know him again first.

They approached the office, and she led him around back to the private entrance. He followed her up the few steps to the front door and paused.

"Do you want to come in for a cup of coffee or a drink?" she asked while fishing for her keys.

He did, but he had other plans. "Thanks anyway, but I need to get up early."

She shrugged, a "suit yourself" gesture, but he saw the hurt and lack of understanding in her gaze.

He reached out and cupped her cheek, his thumb caressing the soft skin in broad strokes. "Do you have plans tomorrow?"

"I'm off. I'm forwarding patients to a covering doctor in the next town. If I don't get some time to myself, I won't be good for anyone." She spoke quickly, obviously in a rush to get inside and away from him.

"How about I pick you up early and we head into Boston for some holiday shopping?" he asked.

She turned to face him. The glow from the outside light illuminated her blond hair and exquisitely made-up features. He hadn't thought about it before, but not only had she shown up at the party, she'd gone all out for it too.

Pleasure took hold inside him. "You're beautiful, you know. Not in the young-girl way I remembered, but in a womanly way I appreciate so much more."

She narrowed her gaze. "What kind of game are you playing, Dylan? You can't come in for a drink because you have plans; then you offer to pick me up early tomorrow. What's going on with you?" Thoroughly annoyed, she perched her hands on her hips while her lips puckered into a pretty pout.

He shook his head. "Sorry about the mixed signals. I want nothing more than to come in, but we both know where that'll lead, and I can't believe I'm saying this, but I want to take it slow."

"Slow?" Her lips mouthed the word. "Ten years isn't slow enough? You'd rather just torture me, is that it?"

"I want you to go to sleep and dream of nothing but me?" He let his fingers trace the outline of her glossed lips. "So when I pick you up tomorrow, you're ready to focus solely and completely on getting to know me again, and me getting to know you."

"You want to discover what makes me tick now?" she asked, a sparkle and teasing glint in her eyes.

"In a word, yes."

Unexpectedly, her tongue darted out and licked the pad of his thumb, being deliberately seductive. He felt the sensation straight through to his already hard groin.

Before he could think it through, he slipped his hand around the back of her neck and pulled her towards him, capturing her mouth with his. Her lips softened but didn't part. Obviously she intended to make him work for what he wanted, and that was okay with him.

He slid his lips back and forth over hers, floored by the gratification he found in tasting her at last. The longer they kissed, the more he realized that his memories had grown fuzzy and reality was so much better and definitely hotter. He braced her face in his hands, tilted her head and continued to tease and taste, just as he'd promised, kissing her slowly, intent on branding her and making sure that if she slept, her dreams would be of him.

His tongue glided over the seam of her lips, and he was rewarded with a low moan from the back of her throat as she opened her mouth and let him inside. He savored the absolute sweetness and desire flooding him. His groin pushed hard against his jeans, the urge to possess her with his body strong.

Before he could go back on his word and join her inside, he stepped back, reminding himself that he wanted to win her trust for the long haul. Not just for one night in bed.

She met his gaze with heavy-lidded eyes, her mouth reddened from his kiss. "You've perfected your technique," she murmured.

He grinned. "I'll take that as a compliment, babe, and you should know, your technique's gotten pretty good too. Still, I don't think technique has anything to do with it."

"No? Then what explains two people who don't learn from their mistakes?"

"Speak for yourself. I've learned a lot from the past. And I think it's *us* that's so potent."

She raised an eyebrow. "This from the man who said we were nothing more than a high-school crush?"

He accepted the blow. "An immature boy said that, not the man I am now."

She swallowed hard. "Who is that man, and what does he want from me?" she asked.

"Time will tell." He didn't mean to be cryptic, but he could hardly say, *I've come back for you*, and expect her to believe his words when his promise had failed her before. "Just give me some time."

Her fingers touched her moist, red lips. "Sex wasn't enough before."

"We're older and wiser now."

She grinned. "We can always hope." She let herself into the apartment and shut the door behind her.

He expelled a breath and tried to pull himself together. He'd been her first, Dylan remembered, and though she'd been an eager learner, she'd rarely initiated sex. This teasing side of her was new, and he liked it a whole lot.

He couldn't wait to explore more.

THREE

Holly knew she'd either lost her mind or she was experiencing an early midlife crisis. There was no other explanation for kissing Dylan and then agreeing to spend more time with him. Then again, what choice did she have? The clean break they'd taken—make that the clean break he'd forced on her—hadn't accomplished anything. Their chemistry and connection was still as strong as ever. She had no choice but to play this through to whatever conclusion awaited her, or she couldn't move on with her life. She'd be in the same limbo hell she'd been in for the last ten years.

So by the time he rang her doorbell the following morning, she was dressed in her favorite jeans and baseball cap and she was ready to shop in Boston with Dylan by her side.

She opened the door, and he greeted her with a cup of Starbucks in each hand. "You come bearing gifts?" she asked, laughing.

"Straight up for me and a froufrou drink for you. I can't think of a better way to take the T to Copley," he said, speaking of Boston's version of public transportation.

"I must've heard you wrong. America's heartthrob is going to take the train? Do you want to get mobbed?" She shook her head, realizing she really hadn't thought about his ego or what his lifestyle must be like now. "Never mind. To be so successful, you must like the spotlight."

He shrugged, looking uncomfortable. "*Like* isn't the right word. It comes with the territory of being successful. You get used to it, but you don't ever enjoy not having a personal life or having to work for a solitary moment."

She studied his serious face. "You don't enjoy the fame?" she asked, surprised.

"I did in the beginning. But it got old fast, and I realized that no matter how many people surrounded me, I was always alone. And lonely."

The wistful sound in his voice caught her off guard and she narrowed her gaze. "Should I pull out the violin?"

He laughed at that. "I'm not looking for your pity. I'm just answering your question and telling it like it is. I want you to know me. Who I was and who I've become. Yes, I love my career, but I've given up a lot for it." Again he sobered as he spoke.

She met his serious stare and suddenly wondered if his return could have more to do with his emotional state than a brief visit to see his mother. He seemed so reflective. But she couldn't imagine that Dylan had suddenly decided that he missed home and Holly. Not after a silent ten years. Which brought up the question, just where did she fit into the equation of his life?

"We all make choices," she said of his decision to pursue a Hollywood career.

"And sometimes we live to regret them." He squeezed her hand, and she felt as if her heart were being clenched tight as well.

"Are you saying you're sorry you went to L.A.?"

He shook his head. "I'm sorry for how I went about it."

She swallowed hard and nodded, not certain she was ready for any further discussion on their past, yet she wasn't ready to end the talk just yet. "And now?"

He grinned. "Now we go about taking things one step at a time. We're going shopping, and we're going to take the train like regular people. Nobody's going to expect to see me on the T, so they'll think maybe I share a resemblance with the famous Dylan North, but they'll be so sure they're wrong they'll leave us alone." He wagged his eyebrows like a kid. "That's what I want. How about you?"

"That's what I want too." That's what scared her so much, she thought as she picked up her ski jacket and her bag. "So who are you shopping for today?"

"I'm a big brother," he explained. And during their trip to the city, he told her about Darrell, the kid he mentored, and the program he'd been funding with a percentage of his earnings for the last two years.

In Sports Authority he purchased a pair of Reebok basketball sneakers, a Spalding official NBA basketball, and some gym clothes for Darrell. Then he ordered basketballs in bulk for a youth program and arranged to have everything shipped to a community center in South Central L.A. Watching the care he took in choosing the gifts, Holly learned that the man wasn't just rich and famous, but he gave back to the community in which he lived, and it became even harder to rein in her heart.

Over lunch he changed the subject. He wanted to hear about her years in college and medical school, which she managed to condense into a short story since she wanted to hear more about him.

He told her about his trip and all his firsts in L.A. She learned about his initial glimpse of the Hollywood sign, his search for an agent and his first job waiting tables, a job from which he was fired for spilling iced tea down Dolly Parton's dress. Laughing, he insisted on paying the check.

While she shopped for family and friends, he revisited his excitement over his first acting job, when he learned which actors would take him under their wing and which were too afraid of losing their own success to help someone else. For the first time she was able to put her hurt aside and see what he'd been searching for as an actor.

She understood they still needed to talk about how he'd handled his decision to leave her, but for now she was content to enjoy his company in an adult way they'd never experienced before. They parted for half an hour, during which she bought his gift. By the time they'd gotten back home, he'd managed to avoid crowds and had signed only two autographs the entire day. Each time someone recognized him, they made a quick escape and found an entirely new place to shop. He was as adept at acting pleased to meet his fans as he was at ducking them at first opportunity.

Holly couldn't remember a more fun or sexually charged day. His cologne turned her on and kept her aroused with each breath she took, and he never stopped touching her. Either he held her hand as they walked, his palm tucked against hers, or he cupped the small of her back, steering her this way and that. Whatever they did, he made certain they were connected the entire afternoon, and as a result, her body tingled with awareness.

At the train station in Acton, they slid into the car and Dylan turned towards her, one hand over her headrest. "So what next?"

Holly's heart pounded hard in her chest. She'd wrestled with this all afternoon, wondering if she could really have Dylan in her apartment and still be the same when he returned to L.A. Probably not, but it didn't matter. Given the chance to be with him, how could she turn him away?

Her gaze met his. "I still have to finish decorating my tree. I could make you dinner in exchange for your help," she offered.

If he turned down this not-so-subtle invitation as he had turned her down last night, she was finished playing his getting-to-know-each-other-again game.

He reached a hand out and caressed her cheek. "I'd love that," he said, the smile on his face evident in his voice.

Tremors of excitement shot through her, and as he turned the engine over, her stomach rolled with anticipation at the night to come.

* * *

Whoever said you couldn't come home again didn't know Holly Evans, Dylan thought. Her apartment was cozy and made him feel welcome and at ease. While she put something together for dinner, Dylan kept himself busy stringing the lights on her tree. He couldn't believe the Holly he knew, who loved Christmas, hadn't decorated her apartment before now, but her hectic schedule was his gain. He put his own touches on her tree, and in doing so he hoped he was making a definite mark in her life.

He heard her footsteps as she walked in to join him. His gaze was immediately drawn to the way the tight denim jeans molded to her hips and thighs. Still slender, she'd filled out in a womanly way that made him hard just looking at her. It wasn't desire alone that beckoned to him but the sense of fulfillment and belonging he found only with her.

Today had shown him that his memories were but shadows of reality. Together they could share so much, if he could convince her to open her heart to him again.

"Hi, there," he said.

"Hi. Dinner should be ready in about forty-five minutes. I hope you like frozen lasagne because when I offered to cook, I forgot I hadn't been shopping in a while. We're lucky I was able to find something to defrost so we could eat at all." She knelt down and sat on the hardwood floor.

"I'd have been happy to take you out, but I'm happier to have more time alone." He patted the empty space beside him, but she kept her distance.

She smiled, but after a day of laughter and relaxed fun, he recognized forced cheer when he saw it. "What's wrong?"

She glanced down, rubbing her palms against her jeans. "I just had some time to think, and I can't help but have questions. A lot of them, actually."

"Like?" he asked, prepared to deal with whatever was on her mind.

She lifted her gaze to meet his. "Like why you left so suddenly and why you came back into my life the same way."

He nodded slowly, glancing up at the empty tree top, wondering where to begin. Hoping he wouldn't push her further away.

Though she sat cross-legged on the floor next to him, their easy camaraderie was gone, and she went out of her way to make sure her bent knee didn't touch his. She was waiting for an explanation, and he wondered if anything he said would make sense—or make a difference to her now.

"You know how badly I wanted to act."

She nodded. "You said Broadway. We had plans. Dreams. At least I thought we did, but after you took off, I convinced myself they'd been *my* dreams and you'd humored me through high school before moving on." At times she even thought that he'd used her, Holly thought.

She bit down on her lower lip, not wanting Dylan to see the extent to which he'd hurt her. Certainly she didn't want him to know his betrayal had probably ruined any chance she had at trusting any other guy. Now that she was beginning to understand how deeply he still affected her, in a way she resented him even more.

He gazed at the needles on the tree as if they could offer clarity until finally he spoke. "The closer we got to graduation, the more trying for Broadway and acting in New York seemed like a sacrifice," he admitted. "Like I'd be accepting second choice without even trying for the big-time."

"So why didn't you just tell me? Or was I that much of a burden?" she asked, admitting her fears out loud for the first time. "Were you afraid I'd hold you back?"

He jerked backward and stared. "Are you serious? It was just the opposite. I didn't want to hold *you* back. Your family had dreams and goals for you. *You* had those same dreams."

Then, at the same time, they both said, "Yale, like your father and his father before him," laughing despite the serious conversation.

"You see? I knew if I told you I wanted to go to L.A., you'd probably have insisted on going with me. Yes, there was Stanford or other schools, but none of them were Yale, and none would uphold your family tradition."

"Wasn't that my choice to make? Unless it was an excuse and you really didn't want me—"

He grasped her hand hard. "I didn't want you to end up resenting me. And in case you need a reminder or proof of how much I did and still do care, here it is." Taking her by surprise, he leaned over and met her lips in a searing, demanding kiss.

A kiss she both wanted and needed, and this time she didn't hesitate. She parted her lips and allowed him inside. His tongue swirled in her mouth, teasing, tasting and demanding she understand. And though she still held the pain in her heart, a part of her accepted the explanation. His kiss and gentle touch went a long way towards helping her heal.

She placed her hands on his shoulders and pushed backward. He toppled to the floor, pulling her on top of him until they lay sprawled beneath her Christmas tree, her legs tangled with his. Their bodies fit tightly yet perfectly together, the hard ridge of his erection thrusting upward against her, making her very aware of his desire, which found a feminine answer inside her.

She couldn't deny the aching emptiness only he could fill or the trickle of desire dampening her panties. She wanted him. Scarier yet, she needed him.

He stared up at her, his sexy gaze smoldering with raw passion and emotion she couldn't mistake. "I missed you, Holly."

"I missed you too," she admitted, and then, to keep things light, she nipped at his lips with soft kisses and teasing strokes of her tongue.

His hands came to rest at her waist. "I told you why I left. Don't you want to know why I came back?"

She trembled, and desire wasn't the reason. "I'm really not sure I want to know. I can't imagine with all that's happened in your life that you just couldn't stop thinking of me," she said, forcing a laugh.

"I couldn't stop thinking of you."

Her heart filled with warmth. "You always knew how to make me feel special, Dylan." But common sense told her not to read too much into his comment.

He'd come home to visit, the first time since she'd been back home, and he came to see her in order to make amends. The chemistry was just a bonus he'd opted to act on, and she certainly hadn't said no. She didn't fault him for that, and she didn't fault herself for letting him back into her life. She needed closure in order to move on. Being with Dylan was giving her that now.

"I can charm anyone. That's a fact." He winked, and she saw the movie star America adored. "But not you. I never could bullshit you, and I don't intend to try and start now."

"Well, good. Then we both understand you came back to set things right between us."

He nodded. "That's one way of putting it."

And there was the probability that he meant his words at face value. That he was home for a short time only. Long enough to make things right and leave his mark, but short enough that he wouldn't get bored. For certain he'd be gone before the itch to move on set in.

Knowing that, she wouldn't mind getting all of Dylan North that she could. "I think we've done enough talking, don't you?" she asked, feeling a wicked grin take hold as she lowered her face to his.

"For now," he agreed.

She nuzzled his neck, her cheek rubbing against his and her lower body beginning to shift from side to side, seeking to increase the building desire and friction between them.

No sooner had she let out a low groan than he flipped her onto her back, switching positions. When they'd been together before, he'd always taken the lead. She was content to let him do so now, certain her time would come to show him how she'd changed and how she'd become more certain of herself and her sexuality.

He pulled her shirt upward, exposing her midriff, his eager hands branding her with their heat as he worked his way upward to her lace bra. His fingertips teased beneath the elastic, his palms finally coming to rest where they belonged, cupping her breasts in his hands.

"You've filled out," he said, approval and gruff desire in his tone.

"Like you'd remember."

His expression changed, his features taking on a wounded look. "You think I don't?"

Unwilling to kill the moment with talk of the women who'd come in between, she shook her head. "I was joking. I remember everything between us, and I'm sure you do too."

His gaze softened. He pulled her top up and over her head, then slipped her bra straps down her shoulders so that he revealed her bare breasts to his hungry gaze.

Shockingly, she felt no embarrassment, only a sense of rightness as he devoured her with one look. His thumbs brushed insistently over her nipples, back and forth, until they hardened into tight peaks and she felt the languorous pull straight to her core. He dipped his head and began a steady suckling with his mouth, his teeth lightly grazing, his tongue gently soothing, but every motion carefully orchestrated to bring her higher and higher, closer to the brink of orgasm.

She wanted his dark head bent at her chest and his warm breath and heat on her breasts as she came apart in his arms. And then she wanted him to fill her completely, so when he left this time she had adult memories to tuck away with the teenage ones she remembered.

"You always knew exactly how to make me come," she murmured, whispering into his hair as his mouth continued to work ultimate magic.

He chuckled and she felt the vibration throughout her body. "That's because you're so damn responsive." And as if to prove his point, he blew a wisp of air across her breasts, the cool breeze puckering her nipples and causing her hips to shift restlessly beneath his.

"See?" He splayed his hand across her belly. "And if I do this, you'll be moaning in no time." His fingertips teased beneath the waistband of her jeans, lightly brushing the triangle of hair just waiting for his touch.

"Dylan," she whispered, her body his for the taking.

"I hear you, babe." He reached for the snap on her jeans at the same time she sought to release his confined erection.

But the jarring ring of his cell phone interrupted them. "I don't want to answer it," he muttered.

The doctor in her disagreed. "Just make sure it's not an emergency."

He rolled off her and groaned, grabbing for his phone. "Hello," he barked into his cell. "Mmm-hmm," he said, then listened some more. "Exactly what I'm looking for." More listening and then, "I'll be there."

His voice rose in definite pleasure, and she wondered if it was a role or a part in a movie he was talking about. She wondered too how preoccupied he'd be now that something big had obviously come up.

"Anything important?" she asked after he'd snapped his phone shut and rolled over to face her, head propped against his hand.

"Just some things I have in the works," he said vaguely, his eyes twinkling.

"Sounds exciting."

He reached over and rubbed his finger across her bottom lip. "Not as exciting as what I want to do with you," he said and pulled her beneath him again.

FOUR

Before Dylan could pick up where they'd left off, Holly jumped up and headed for the kitchen to pull the lasagne from the oven to let it cool a bit before dinner. He took the few minutes alone to evaluate things between them so far.

He knew he'd made progress with Holly, but not enough for her to believe in a future. Certainly not enough to tell her that the phone call had been from a real estate agent who'd found him five acres of wooded land and the perfect setting to build a house not far from Acton. Dylan had reached a point where he was ready to settle down away from the insanity that was Hollywood. With or without Holly in his life, he planned to purchase property and make it his permanent home between movie shoots.

They'd already talked about his reasons for leaving and coming back now, but she was still skittish and unwilling to trust emotionally. He didn't mind starting by winning over her body in the hopes that her heart and mind would soon follow.

He paused in her bedroom and returned with a blanket, spreading it out over the floor in the family room and waiting until Holly came out of the kitchen.

"Did we ever make love beneath the Christmas tree?" he asked her.

Instead of bolting or growing wary, a slow, sexy smile curved her lips. "Not that I recall. We'd have been too afraid of getting caught."

"There's no one to catch us now," he deliberately hinted.

"You don't say." She stepped towards him, an extra wiggle in her hips. He couldn't mistake the fact that she remained half-dressed in her jeans, bra and nothing else. She hadn't opted to dress or cover herself, another good sign.

He sat back and waited.

"So if I were to undress right here, no one would mind?" she asked, becoming a teasing seductress in front of his eyes.

Before he could reply, she tipped her head to one side, and as he watched, she reached for and released the front clasp of her bra.

His breath caught as she slowly shimmied the straps off her shoulders and pulled the cups away so her full breasts were bare, and he was drooling.

"I sure as hell don't mind," he said, awed by her rounded breasts, flat stomach and sense of confidence, all of which turned him on.

"Then this won't bother you either." She unsnapped the button on her jeans and lowered the zipper.

He swallowed hard.

Hands at her hips, she eased the waistband down. He didn't know where to focus first, the expanse of pale skin on her stomach or the blond triangle of hair she slowly revealed when she'd hooked her thumbs into her underwear and drawn them down too.

"You're gorgeous," he said, shocked he could formulate a coherent sentence.

She smiled.

Surely this physical trust had to mean he'd made more headway in breaching her barriers than he'd thought. If not, he was going to be one miserable son of a bitch in the morning.

But damn he'd enjoy tonight.

He reached for her, but she playfully smacked at his hand. "No touching until we're equally at risk of being caught naked," she said, laughing.

"If you're asking me to strip, no problem." He grabbed for the fly on his jeans, which had grown way too tight, but she stopped him with one hand.

"I want you to put yourself in *my* hands."

Ironic. He wanted her trust. She was asking for his.

He raised his hands in the air and sucked in a deep breath as she popped the button on his jeans and, with some maneuvering on his part, removed his clothing.

Then she splayed her hands against his chest, her touch warm and inviting. "Did you mean it when you said you'd missed me?"

In her voice, he heard the uncertainty as the sassy seductress warred with the woman who still felt used and left behind.

He twined their fingers together and pulled her onto the blanket. "I missed you," he assured her. "Not a day went by that I didn't think of you."

She moistened her lips. "Me too," she admitted. "Even if it was just in my dreams."

His heart pounding hard in his chest, he leaned over her, his rock-hard erection poised at her moist entrance. He wanted to be inside her more than he wanted to breathe. But he also needed to know she felt and desired the same thing.

"Dylan?"

"Hmm?"

"Show me how much you missed me, because I know I missed you," Holly whispered, telling him exactly what he needed to hear.

He reached down with one hand, teasing her dewy folds, easing first one finger and then another inside her. She arched her back and moaned, and with a shuddering breath, he thrust hard and deep, entering her at last.

He was immediately clasped in her moist heat, her inner walls squeezing him tight. Both the physical and emotional sensations were stronger than any he could ever remember, and his pulse beat hard in his throat as he lost any semblance of coherent thought.

As Dylan stilled inside her, Holly's breath caught and she lay motionless, adjusting to his size and length, to the exquisite feel of him, hard and rigid inside her, where he belonged. She clenched him tighter, and the pulling sensation grew, spiraling and taking her to dizzying new heights.

He met her gaze and withdrew slowly, so she felt every hard ridge of his desire until suddenly she was empty and aching without him. "Dylan, please." She arched, trying to pull him back inside her again.

"Happy to, babe," he said and thrust with his hips, his hard erection filling her and making her whole once more.

She let out a sob of gratitude, unable to hide her emotions.

"Feels so right, doesn't it?" he asked, his voice gruff.

She could manage only a low moan from deep in her throat.

He chuckled, but his body trembled, his control obviously stretched to the breaking point. So was hers. She lifted her legs, pulling her knees backward and drawing him inexorably deeper inside her body, until they were so close, she couldn't imagine they were anything but one. And then with a groan, he released his tenuous control and began to grind against her, moving and pumping his hard body into hers.

Their connection was electric, their movements synchronized and perfect, as if they had an unspoken understanding of each other's bodies and needs. Her fingers gripped his back as she gasped for breath, shuddering and coming closer and closer to coming apart. She didn't think he could get any deeper, doubted she could *feel* any more emotion, when she instinctively hooked her ankles together behind his back. Locked in place, he rolled his hips against hers, grinding at the same time he found the perfect spot and her body shattered from inside out. Her orgasm hit hard, and she rode it out to its conclusion, her climax wringing everything out of her.

Just then he took her off guard and shifted positions. She caught on and helped until he lay flat on his back and she was astride him. She hadn't thought she could move or that another orgasm was possible, but when he shifted his hips beneath her, she changed her mind. The rhythmic rotation of his pelvis and the intimate contact of her feminine mound against his body had the contractions starting all over again.

"Do it," he told her. "Make me come," he said, his hands gripping her waist tight.

She did as he asked and took control, shifting her hips from side to side, lifting her body up and down over his, so he moved in and out at *her* whim. And it seemed that was what he'd been waiting for before he let himself go too.

His orgasm was explosive, his body practically slamming upward into hers and making her peak a second time. But now she forced her eyes open and watched him as he came, eyes shut tight, jaw clenched and lost in shared pleasure and ecstasy, and it was all she could do not to cry and let her overwhelming emotions betray her.

He fell back against the floor, his hands still on her waist, as sated and exhausted as she. She collapsed against him, their breathing coming together in rapid gulps. His heart pounded against her forehead, and she swallowed hard, fighting back the feelings he'd inspired. The overwhelming love she felt for this man frightened her because she did still love him. Had probably never stopped.

He completed her, she realized now, and as he held her tight, she wondered if this moment together would be one of their last. Because he'd never be satisfied in Acton, the small town with its slow pace and lack of excitement. The town he'd happily left behind once before.

* * *

A quick kiss, no explanation, and Dylan left first thing the next morning. Holly told herself she was glad, that things had played out as she'd expected. She told herself she could handle the brief fling he obviously wanted and intended. And she'd keep telling herself that until she believed her own words.

She stopped at the office to do some insurance paperwork and see a few sick patients, before heading to the grocery store to fill her empty refrigerator and the department store for gifts. Christmas carols played over the speakers in the supermarket as she loaded her cart. As usual, the store was the central meeting place, and more than one friendly face commented on Dylan's return and how his car had been parked on her street late into the night.

Her face flushed hot with the first remark, and she was certain her cheeks remained pink as she went up and down the aisles. By the time she reached the checkout line and pushed her cart behind Dylan's mother of all people, she was sure she had reached her maximum state of mortification.

"Holly, honey, how are you?" Kate asked, as she placed her items onto the belt.

"Just fine. And you?"

"Good. Good," she said, smiling. "About Dylan—"

"Yes?" Holly asked warily.

Because of her relationship with Dylan and all the time she'd spent with his family, she and his mother had remained close after he'd gone. By unspoken agreement though, they'd never discussed Dylan. Apparently that was about to change.

"I'm so happy you and my son have made your peace." Kate beamed, obviously unfazed that Dylan had been out all night at Holly's.

But Holly was even more humiliated than before. Not once last night had she given small-town gossip a thought, and since she and Dylan were both adults, she certainly hadn't been thinking that his mother would notice his absence.

She gripped the cart handle tighter, her knuckles white as she tried to acknowledge Kate's comment without embarrassing herself further. "We've come to an understanding," she said diplomatically.

Better than admitting Dylan had spent the night in her bed, his big body wrapped around hers, his hands doing all sorts of sinful, erotic things to her. And she had more than reciprocated, relearning his body, what he liked, what he loved and what really turned him on.

She shivered and forced a smile for his mother's sake.

Kate continued talking. "I told Dylan I expected you both for dinner tomorrow night. It is Christmas Eve, after all."

Before Dylan's return, Nicole had invited her over but she hadn't decided whether she'd rather be alone. "That's sweet but I'm not sure what my plans are yet," Holly hedged. She and Dylan hadn't made any more plans to see each other, and she didn't want his choices to be influenced by his mother's command.

But Kate waved a hand, dismissing Holly's words. "Your mother would never forgive me if I left you alone on the holiday when she was with her sister. Besides, look at all the food in the cart. I'll cook all day tomorrow. Dylan's already agreed, so it's settled."

Holly inhaled deeply and let the decision be made for her. "Then at least let me bring dessert."

"Nonsense, honey. You just spend time with Dylan and let me worry about dinner. Just bring yourself around four. Okay?"

"Okay," she said, knowing she'd bring *something* anyway. "I look forward to it." Which was true. She'd love to spend the holiday with Dylan and his family.

She just hoped Dylan felt the same way.

* * *

Dylan returned from his meeting with the real estate agent on an all-time high. He'd found the perfect parcel of land and had already made an offer. If he closed his eyes, he could envision exactly the kind of house he wanted to build there. He returned to Holly's, whistling as he rang the bell and waited for her to answer.

She opened the door, a smile on her face that widened when she saw him. She wore casual sweats and a pink sweatshirt she'd cut at the arms and across the middle. With her tousled curls and lightly made-up face, she looked delicious, good enough to eat and definitely good enough to come home to every single day.

He grinned and whistled louder.

"Someone's in a good mood," she said.

He stepped inside and swung her through the air before setting her bare feet down on the floor. But not before letting her slide down the length of his body and feel how much he'd missed her. "I'm just enjoying life."

She looked at him curiously, and her gaze narrowed as she studied him. "So just where were you that put you in such a good mood?"

"I was Christmas shopping. For you," he said, teasing her.

"You were out doing something for me?" Her blue eyes twinkled with delight.

"You bet." He debated whether to tell her about the land now or wait to give her her gift until Christmas Eve, like in his dream.

A chimelike ring sounded from the kitchen, drawing his attention. "I didn't realize I left my cell here." He thought he'd left it at his mother's place.

Holly nodded. "It's been ringing all afternoon. I'm guessing voice mail picked it up."

He could hear the withdrawal in her voice, and he rolled his suddenly stiff shoulders. The last thing he needed or wanted was his other life intruding on the headway he'd been making with Holly, but he couldn't afford to be out of touch for too long.

He glanced towards the kitchen. "Let me check the messages and then we can talk, okay?"

She nodded. "Sure. I've got some gifts of my own to wrap," she said with a wink and left him alone.

He grabbed a pen and a sheet of paper and retrieved his messages, jotting down notes of who'd called. Then he returned the most pressing messages.

Holly entered the kitchen to find Dylan on the phone, pad and paper in front of him. She stepped inside, not wanting to bother him, but he gestured for her to come in, indicating she wasn't intruding on a private conversation.

Still, he was obviously absorbed in the discussion, and as she passed by the table, she saw he was noting figures and names on the paper, then tossing alternative numbers and people back at the person on the other end of the phone. He was animated and engaged, and it was obvious to Holly he loved what he did, down to what she assumed was negotiations on starring in a movie.

She was as much intrigued by his business as she was dismayed by the realization that she'd never truly have him. Not if it meant him settling in their small hometown and leaving the glitz, glamour and business of Hollywood behind. If she'd held any illusions or hopes, they were dispelled that instant.

Yet as much as the realization hurt, she'd never want to take something away from him that he loved so much. For the first time she understood what he meant when he said he'd left so she could pursue her dream and not resent him later on. She wouldn't want him to resent her either. She cared too much. So she would gladly take all he offered now and be grateful for this time they shared. A time she intended to make the most of as soon as he got off the phone.

While she waited for him to finish his call, she pulled a jar of Marshmallow Fluff out of the cabinet and a spoon from the drawer. She hopped up on the countertop the way she sometimes did when she was eating in a rush and feasted on her favorite snack.

"Yes, yes, I'll think it over and get back to you," Dylan said, his deep voice interrupting her thoughts. He paused before adding, "No, I'm not calling Melanie back. My decision about this has nothing to do with whether *she* takes the lead female role."

Holly's stomach jumped at the mention of the other woman's name. She scooped a heaping teaspoonful of Marshmallow Fluff and stuffed it into her mouth for good measure.

Meanwhile Dylan groaned. "Can you call Harry for me? I don't care how much he hates you, I pay you to run interference," he said and finally clicked off, ending the call.

"My agent," he said, turning her way. He shot her an apologetic look. "Sorry about that. It took longer than I thought."

She shrugged. "It's business. I understand."

He rose and strode over to where she sat. "Do you picture me as a superhero?" he asked.

"Would you have to wear tights?"

He laughed. "Why? Do you have a problem with my legs?"

"Nope." They were as strong and powerful as the rest of him. But something told her that despite their banter, this wasn't a lightly asked question. Rather, he was asking her opinion on his next role. "Wasn't your last film more serious?"

"You saw *Last Dawn*?"

She forced a nod. Hard as it was to admit, she'd seen all his movies. She made it a point to go alone to the theater in order to spare herself questions, comments and innuendo from her friends.

"My guess is that now you're worried if you go back to an action film or one based on a comic book character, you'll be taking a step backward when it comes to being taken more seriously as an actor."

"How'd you know?" he asked, surprise evident in his tone. Yet by the warm smile and gleam in his eyes, he was obviously pleased she understood his concerns without him having to explain.

"I watched the evolution of your work." She stated the truth for his benefit alone. Admitting she'd followed his career made her feel even more vulnerable to him than she already was.

"And what'd you think?" A muscle ticked in his jaw as he leaned against the counter beside her.

She wondered if the insecurity she sensed was a figment of her imagination or if he really cared about what she thought of his work.

She placed the jar down on the counter, pushing it out of the way. "*Last Dawn* was a real stretch," she said of his portrayal of a convict on death row. "You showed depth and range. Real growth."

"And?" he asked, correctly sensing she wasn't through critiquing him yet.

"And taking a commercial role now could damage the new reputation you're seeking to establish."

He leaned forward, his forehead close to hers. "You're suggesting I turn it down?"

She drew a deep breath, finding it hard to believe he'd need her opinion on something so important. "I'm saying you should think long and hard before agreeing. And—"

"And?" he asked, grinning.

"And the possibility of Melanie Masterson playing opposite you has nothing to do with that suggestion," she said, forcing the words out on a rush of air.

He tipped his head backward and let loose with a genuine laugh. "Nothing to do with it?"

She shoved his shoulder with one hand, hating that he'd caught her feeling any jealousy at all. "Almost nothing," she said.

"You need to know she was a fling," he told her.

"A long-lasting one though." She couldn't help but state facts and hope he'd fill her in some more.

He tipped his head to one side, studying her. "I was searching for something, trying to pretend she could fill a void…" His voice trailed off.

His words reminded her of her own feelings about John and a distinct wave of guilt arose. She tamped it down. John had given her this time to figure things out, and from the look on his face, he already knew where her heart lay. She sighed and pushed thoughts of John out of her head, at least for a few more days. She'd promised herself this time and she needed to take it.

Meanwhile, Dylan sat waiting for her reply. "I get it more than you know," she murmured. "As for the movie, you have to know my opinion doesn't mean a thing. I don't know the business or the players. I don't even know how important commercial success is to you."

In short, Holly thought, she was on the outside of his life looking in. She felt like a complete fraud offering her opinion at all.

He stepped between her legs, his face inches from hers. "I beg to differ, babe."

His words caught her up short. "Why?"

"Because of all the people in this world, you know me. You get me. My agent was clicking his teeth at the money involved, and my publicist would kill to work on a project like this." He frowned, a testament to how few people in his inner circle had his own interests completely at heart.

"And it goes without saying that Melanie would like to lasso me and drag me kicking and screaming to the studio lot since it suits her needs. So I have no one to turn to except myself. And you. If I didn't want or trust your judgment, I wouldn't have asked."

"Oh." Her mouth had grown dry at his admission.

Her heart squeezed tight at the possibility that just maybe he was placing her in a position of importance in his life. She was too afraid to ask.

She'd rather reach out and enjoy *now* as she'd promised herself she'd do. And with him settled between her thighs, his lips inches from hers, he was in a prime position for her to do exactly that.

FIVE

Dylan had noticed the uncertainty in Holly's eyes from the moment she joined him in the kitchen. It wasn't him she mistrusted but the lure of his career. That's what had taken him away from her before. Damned if he knew how to convince her that she was exactly what he needed, not just in his life as a friend, but an integral part of it.

He didn't have time to think, let alone talk, any more, not when she was linking her ankles behind his back and pulling him deeper into the vee of her legs. Though the rational part of him knew she was using sex to escape serious discussion, desire flooded him, the need to be inside her again all-consuming.

"Holly," he said, trying to refocus her thoughts as well as his.

"Dylan," she mimicked, her hands sliding into the waistband of his jeans.

She pushed herself forward on the counter until she sat at the very edge and he was nestled between her thighs. He couldn't mistake her intent or her need. The warmth and heat emanating from her body called to him in a primitive way he couldn't mistake. His body throbbed, his erection thrusting against his jeans, and suddenly discussion could definitely wait.

Eyes glittering, she met his gaze. "You were saying?"

He shook his head. "It'll keep." His surprise would make a better gift given at the right time.

"I thought so. Now, how about letting me have my wicked way with you?" Her lips turned upward in a seductive grin.

He still wasn't used to this teasing side of her, but he sure liked it. "What'd you have in mind?"

She hopped down from the counter, and with deft hands, she opened his jeans. As he watched, his breath coming in shorter and shorter gasps, she pulled the denim over his hips and thighs. When they reached his ankles, he kicked the pants aside. His briefs quickly followed, and his freed erection sprang to life.

Pulse pounding, heart racing, he met her gaze. "What now?"

She patted the counter where she'd once sat. "Have a seat."

He complied, shivering when the Formica touched his bare skin. "Damn, that's cold."

"Don't worry. I have every intention of warming you," she said, her voice hot and thick. "Do you remember what my favorite ice cream topping is?"

He raised an eyebrow. "I'm guessing it's still that Marshmallow Fluff you were just eating."

She reached for the jar and brought it beside him. He glanced from the gooey white fluff to the wicked gleam in her eyes. "You wouldn't," he said, the blood rushing in his ears at the very thoughts soaring through his head.

"You don't think I would?" She dabbed her finger into the jar and slowly placed it into her mouth, sucking the crème from her finger with her tongue, grazing with her teeth, all her movements deliberately, seductively slow.

His erection throbbed harder and his mouth grew dry.

"Well?" she asked.

"I dare you," he said, using the words that had once provoked her into sneaking out of her house to meet him by the corner of her street so they could go make out in his car.

She met and held his stare for a brief moment before dipping her fingers into the jar. Drawing a deep breath, she coated the head of his erect penis with the Fluff. He'd wanted to watch, but as her fingers and the sticky substance touched his aching member, the sensation was too much. He leaned his head back against the cabinets and groaned aloud, knowing he was powerless and completely at her mercy.

Forcing his eyes open, he noticed that Holly was trembling, perhaps even more than Dylan, which told him a lot. Despite the playful teasing, she was deadly serious about him. He knew it in his gut.

Lowering her head, she bent and took him into her mouth, drawing him in deep. The moist warmth was nearly his undoing. He nearly came then, before she even began working him, but he managed to exercise control. He gripped the edge of the countertop hard with his fingertips, his head still resting against the cabinets, his body shaking with a restraint that lasted only until she began a steady, rhythmic sucking.

Her tongue licked the Fluff, licking at *him*, pulling, teasing up and down. She grazed the head of his penis with gentle teeth, then soothed long, luxurious laps of her tongue, never letting up. He was shaking even before his climax hit, and when it did, the sensation rocked him hard, wave after wave consuming him. Lost in the world she created, he came. And carne. And came.

When he'd caught his breath, he opened his eyes to find her staring back at him. He cupped her head in his hands and looked into her warm, giving eyes.

"I love you, babe." He'd meant to kiss her. The words toppled out instead.

She straightened and took a step back. Dylan realized his mistake immediately. He'd spoken too soon, and he'd shaken her up badly. But before he could say a word to smooth things over, the telephone rang and she dove to answer it.

Cursing, he jumped down and pulled on his pants. He wanted to deal with her fully dressed and fix his mistake as quickly as possible before she withdrew even further.

Unfortunately, she returned from the phone call, reaching for her purse. "It's an emergency. I have to go."

She'd turned from his seductress to shaken woman to in-control doctor in seconds flat. He respected it. Respected her.

"Let me drive you." For selfish reasons he didn't want to be apart from her right now.

She gave a curt nod. "I don't have time to argue. Robert Hansen's five-year-old fell and hit his head on the corner of a table. He's got a huge gash, and there's lots of blood. I said I'd meet them at the hospital."

"Good thing I got dressed," he said, laughing.

Unfortunately, she didn't join in.

* * *

Holly had never been happy at someone else's expense and she wasn't about to start feeling that way now, but she couldn't deny she'd been so darn grateful for the phone call that had distracted her from Dylan's heartfelt words. Her heart pounded hard in her chest even now, as she filled out the last of the paperwork on Jason Hansen. The child had received stitches and had just narrowly missed hitting his eye on the table corner in his fall. He was one lucky little boy, she thought, signing her name and handing the clipboard in at the hospital desk.

Dylan waited for her in the lounge, where she'd have to face him and their shared afternoon. She'd started by using sex and foreplay as a distraction. A means of avoiding more serious discussion that might lead to him telling her he needed to return to L.A. But her deliberately seductive move had turned into a completely emotional one for her.

She'd wanted to give to him in a way he couldn't possibly forget. She wanted to be indelibly etched in his mind forever just as she knew that moment would be a permanent part of her, heart and soul. And now she had to live with the consequences.

She didn't doubt he loved her. It was his ability to do anything about his feelings that she didn't trust. His work would take him away from her, and the lifestyle in L.A. couldn't possibly compete with small-town life in Acton, Massachusetts. Sure, he said he was tired of the throngs of people and fans, tired of the phoniness in his world, but he'd wither and die here. And she refused to be the reason or the one he grew to resent.

Steeling herself for any discussion he might want to have, she walked back towards the small waiting room and strode through the double doors. There must have been a lull in traffic because the room was empty except for Dylan, who'd curled into the corner of the plastic couch and dozed off. A lock of his hair had fallen over his forehead, and his head rested against his balled-up leather jacket.

Her heart turned over at the sight, and she knelt down next to the couch. "Hey, sleepyhead." She nudged his arm and tried to wake him, but he'd always been a deep sleeper, so it took a few more tries before he finally jerked his head upward.

"Hey." He rubbed his eyes with his palms. "Are you all finished?"

She nodded.

"How's the kid?"

"Other than a few stitches, he's really lucky. But I doubt he'll be in the mood to wrestle with his brothers anytime soon."

Dylan laughed. "He's lucky to have you as his doctor." His voice sobered, and Holly sensed his serious mood, return. "I watched you in action, you know."

Embarrassed, she shook her head. "Once I get started in an emergency, I don't see much else around me."

"I realized that." Holly's dedication and abilities hadn't come as a surprise to him, yet his respect for her had grown tremendously. And in an odd way, seeing her work had validated his decision to leave her behind all those years ago.

He rose and stretched out his muscles, which were cramped from being in one position for so long. "Are you ready to head home?"

"Uh, yeah." She seemed surprised.

They walked to the parking lot, and he slipped his arm around her shoulders. "I'm sure you're exhausted."

She nodded. "I could use a hot shower and a good night's sleep."

"Sounds like a definite plan," he murmured, and in case she wasn't sure what he meant, he nuzzled his lips against her neck and whispered what the two of them could do in that shower before she collapsed from exhaustion in her bed. With him by her side.

She laughed with him, her sexy way of agreeing to his idea. But she still seemed wary.

He guessed she was waiting for him to bring up his comment in her kitchen earlier. He didn't plan on doing so. In fact, while alone here waiting, he'd decided to continue on as if nothing unusual had happened between them. He had little time before he had to return to L.A. for a meeting with his agent and a movie producer, which had nothing to do with superhero roles and everything to do with a part he was dying to tackle.

He wished he had the luxury of time to lay things out for Holly a little more slowly and with more care than he'd shown by blurting out his feelings in her kitchen. But what he didn't have in time, they more than made up for in emotional connection. Beyond that, Dylan had no choice but to let fate play itself out.

* * *

After their eventful night, Dylan and Holly slept late. They woke, made love and fell asleep again. The day passed in a delicious way and then they arrived at Dylan's mother's house. Dinner at the Northwood house was just like being back in high school, when life was simple and everything seemed rosy and good, Holly thought. She'd called her mother and aunt to say hi before going over to Dylan's. She missed her mother, but understood her aunt Rose had broken her hip and needed help and so Holly tried not to dwell on the emptiness of being without her own family during the holiday season. And once she arrived at Dylan's house, that emptiness began to be filled.

Dylan's mother had cooked dinner, and the house smelled delicious, warm and inviting. His sister, Amy, and her husband, Tom, and their young son, a precocious three-year-old named Matt, sat in the family room in front of the big-screen television Dylan had purchased for his mother's birthday. Typical males, Dylan and Tom talked football and took turns keeping the fire stoked and the room warm, while Amy and Matt provided the sounds of laughter and squabbling. Amy kept busy diving to keep Matt out of trouble near the hearth and away from an old black Lab that dozed in the corner and whose tail Matt liked to pull.

Holly, after being thrown out of the kitchen for attempting to help, finally settled in beside Dylan, trying desperately not to like the feeling of being part of this family too much. But how could she not enjoy and feel welcome when every so often Dylan would reach out and massage her shoulders or idly twist her hair around his finger as he talked. His family all treated her as if she belonged here, as if she and Dylan had never broken up or been apart.

But most defining for Holly was that here in his old home, Dylan's stardom and fame didn't exist, making it too easy for *her* to believe in a future. So much so that throughout dinner and dessert, she had to keep reminding herself that she'd succumbed to these fantasies once before and suffered nothing but heartache as a result.

By the time Dylan drove her home, she was stuffed from the good food and overwhelmed by memories and desire. When he turned and asked if he could come in, saying yes came as naturally to her as breathing.

Coming on top of the heavy-duty family scene, Dylan wanted to tread carefully now. Holly had relaxed in a way he hadn't seen since his return, and he didn't want to lose that mellow, comfortable mood.

"That was so nice." She dropped the keys onto the shelf in her front hall. "I love your family."

"Well, that's good, because they love you too." His gaze darted to hers, wondering if any version of the word love would put her on edge.

"Can I get you coffee or something to drink?"

He accepted the subject change with a nod. "A cup of coffee sounds great."

"Then make yourself at home." She smiled and gestured to the couch in the family room.

While she headed to make him coffee he didn't really need or want, he readied the room for just one of the surprises he had in store for Holly.

* * *

Thanks to a fast-brewing machine that made four cups of coffee at a time, Holly had coffee ready for herself and Dylan pretty quickly. She knew he liked his black, so she added milk and sugar for herself and walked back into her family room.

Instead of the bright space she'd left behind, Dylan had transformed the room. He'd shut off the overhead lights and turned on a small lamp in the corner along with the multicolored bulbs on her Christmas tree. From her small CD player, uplifting holiday music filled the air around them, while Dylan sat on the couch with a small wrapped box in his hand.

From across the room, she felt the heat of his stare branding her much like his heated touch. God, he was sexy. No doubt every woman who saw a similar pose from the pages of a magazine dreamed of him staring at her, wanting her, only having eyes for *her.*

He was every woman's fantasy, and for this short span of time he belonged to her. She was lucky, but she wasn't deluded by his fame. She had enough self-respect to believe that for as long as Dylan was with her, he was lucky too.

She walked inside and set the cups down on the table. "I like the atmosphere," she said softly, grateful for the thoughtful gesture.

He grinned. "I did the best with what I had." He toyed with the ribbon on the small box, rubbing the satin back and forth between his fingers, in the same way he'd massaged certain parts of her body with gentle yet arousing care.

She swallowed hard, searching for a distraction. "What's in the box?"

"Part of your Christmas gift."

"It's early! I didn't know we were going to exchange gifts tonight. Mine isn't even wrapped yet." She had something special for him when they'd separated the day they'd been in Boston. She hadn't decided when to give it to him.

He stood and grasped her hand, pulling her down beside him on the couch. "I want you to have this and I don't want anything from you in exchange."

"Not even if its the watch you were eyeing in the store window?" She tipped her head to the side and looked at him through not-so-innocent eyes.

He shook his head. "You noticed that? Man, you are something else. Want to know what my—what Melanie got me for Christmas last year?"

She stiffened, but he held on tightly to her hands. "No, but something tells me you're going to tell me anyway."

"She bought me a weekend for two at a spa. Seaweed wraps, facials and full-body massages." He grimaced, his disgust with her gift evident even now, a year later.

Holly burst out laughing, her nerves over the mention of Melanie giving way to complete shock and amusement. "She really doesn't know you at all."

"No, she doesn't. Not like we know each other." He held out the gift box. "It's sentimental, not expensive," he said, his voice dropping low. His tone held a hint of embarrassment.

She couldn't help but smile. "I'm not looking for anything expensive. I wasn't looking for anything at all."

"I know, but this is something I want you to have." He rose and began pacing the room. Obviously something was on his mind, so she set the box aside until he could explain.

"About a month ago, I dreamed about you. Nothing unusual—I always dream about you."

Her breath caught in her throat. "You do?"

"Yeah. That time I dreamed about us exchanging gifts on Christmas Eve, and I was determined to make that dream come true again. As soon as possible."

Despite her resolve to remain strong, her throat swelled and her heart began pounding hard in her chest. "So you really came back for me?"

"I told you I did." He jerked his head towards his gift. "Open it."

She did as he asked, untying the bow and ripping off the paper. The white box was generic without a hint of what was inside. Curious, she pulled off the top and peeked inside. Her breath caught in her throat, and she lifted the gift gently in her hands.

"The angel I bought your family for their tree," she said, memories swamping her. "You're giving it back to me?"

He knelt beside her. "It's all in how you look at things, babe. I want you to hold on to this and think of why I'd give it to you, okay? How it could impact *us*." He took the angel from her hand and placed it on the table.

Then he swept her into his arms and into the bedroom.

* * *

Christmas Day, Holly awoke feeling warm and sated, and she tingled all over. She'd never felt as cherished and cared for as she had when Dylan had made love to her last night.

She closed her eyes and let herself remember. His warm body melding with hers, his eyes warm and giving. Most of all, she recalled the absolute feeling of fulfillment as he came inside her.

She rolled over to glance at the clock on the nightstand but the first thing she saw was her angel instead. They'd never put it on the tree, she thought. That was something they'd get to later on, she hoped, because she already sensed Dylan had left again this morning. Knowing Dylan, since he was home for a short visit, she felt sure he'd gone to see his mother.

She felt just as certain he'd be back.

Lying alone in her bed gave her time to think, maybe for the first time since Dylan's surprise visit to her office. As she let *all* her feelings wash over her, her first thought wasn't of Dylan, but of John. It wasn't so much guilt she felt as a heaviness in her heart because he was a wonderful man. But there would be time to deal with her feelings for John soon enough. Right now, she had a rare morning off and she intended to enjoy it by lounging in bed and not thinking of problems or possible solutions.

She reached for the television remote and turned on one of the morning shows, caught one segment, then dozed through the weather. She woke up again just as an entertainment reporter was dishing on the latest buzz from Hollywood.

She watched the list of stars who celebrated birthdays and heard the latest scandals before a picture on the screen caught Holly's attention. Actress Melanie Masterson's beautiful face flashed before Holly's eyes.

Curious despite herself, and compelled to watch, she sat up straighter in bed and raised the volume.

"Ms. Masterson issued a statement through her publicist announcing a New Year's Day wedding to her on-again, off-again boyfriend, Dylan North," the reporter said.

Holly pulled her knees up and wrapped her arms around her legs.

"Neither Dylan North nor his representative was available for comment, but this reporter happened to see them at a party earlier this year and they were glued together. Whatever caused their breakup obviously wasn't serious enough to keep them apart in the coming year. Diane, back to you."

Holly shook her head. "No way," she said to the television screen.

Melanie might be beautiful, but she didn't understand Dylan, not the way Holly did. And though Dylan loved his career, he wouldn't settle for a shadow of the type of woman he wanted. Then there was the fact that he'd been in Holly's bed last night. Not Melanie's. The other woman obviously had an agenda. Still, Dylan wasn't here with Holly now, and this unsettling news did nothing to relax her.

She'd lost her luxurious morning in bed, and she yanked the comforter down, rose from bed and headed for the kitchen. If nothing else, coffee would get her day back on track.

No sooner had she reached the kitchen than her telephone rang, and she snatched up the receiver. "Hello?"

"Hi, babe."

On hearing Dylan's voice, her spirits soared. "Dylan!"

"Good morning," he said gruffly.

She felt herself smile. "Good morning to you too."

"Do you have any idea how much I wanted to be there when you woke up?"

His deep voice caused a distinct warmth to settle low in her stomach. "I think I can imagine. Why'd you leave so early?"

"I went to see my mother. We have so little time, and I knew she'd appreciate a quick Christmas visit. I planned on being back before you even woke up. But—"

She gripped the receiver tight in her hand. "But what?"

"I got a call and I have to catch a flight to L.A. I'm at the airport now."

Her stomach, which had just fluttered with warmth and desire, now plummeted in disappointment. "Does it have to do with Melanie?" she asked coolly, deliberately keeping any emotion out of her voice.

"Not in the way you think. It has more to do with the movie role."

Holly drew a deep breath and tried to understand. "The role you decided not to take? Or did you change your mind?"

"No, I didn't change my mind, but the director isn't someone I want to alienate, and my agent suggested we meet with him right away and discuss it fare-to-face. When I factor in travel time, I needed to leave today to make the meeting tomorrow."

She nodded. "And Melanie?"

"Wants me to take the role, and she'll do anything to get me back to L.A. to convince me," he said grimly.

"Including announcing a New Year's wedding?" Holly asked.

He muttered a succinct curse. "You know about that?"

"It was on the morning news."

His voice was cut off by an airport announcement. "What did you say?" she asked.

"My plane's boarding. I said to remember what I told you about believing newspaper articles." She heard the pleading tone in his voice.

"I remembered." She let out a strained laugh.

"I have to go, but Holly?"

She shut her eyes and leaned against the wall. "Yeah?"

"I love you, and I *will* be back."

"Bye, Dylan." For Holly, the trick was to find the strength and courage to believe him.

SIX

Holly skipped breakfast and spent the rest of the morning playing Santa, dropping gifts off for friends and family, taking her time before returning home. When the doorbell rang, it caught her by surprise.

"Hi, Nicole." Holly forced a smile.

"That's a really grumpy 'hi' on Christmas! Good thing I came with something to make you smile." Nicole strode inside, carrying a large shopping bag.

"Let's go sit." Holly gestured towards the family room. "I stopped by your apartment, but you weren't home," she said as they settled in.

"That's because I was coming here." Nicole curled her legs Indian style beneath her, making herself at home.

Gesturing to the bag, she said, "I wanted to find a way to thank you for being so good to me since I moved here. So I made you this." She reached into the bag and pulled out a gorgeous, handmade blanket in a variety of earth-tone colors to match Holly's family room.

"Oh I *love* it. Thank you." Holly hugged her friend tight, "That was so thoughtful. I didn't know you knit!"

"My grandmother taught me."

Holly smiled. "Well, I have your present right here." She jumped up and pulled Nicole's gift from beneath her tree. "It's store bought and practical," she said sheepishly. "And nothing as beautiful as this." She fingered the soft wool, curling it between her fingers.

Nicole opened a box and pulled out a Tiffany key ring with her initial. On the key ring was a key to the office. "I thought you'd want more freedom to come and go as you please once you have the title of office manager," Holly said, hoping her friend would be pleased with the gifts.

Nicole's eyes grew wide. "Me? Office manager?"

Holly nodded. "With my new partner starting soon and him bringing in his patients from the next town over, we need a full-fledged manager. I talked to Lance—Dr. Tollgate—and he agreed to a promotion and a raise. Merry Christmas," she told her friend.

Nicole squealed and hugged Holly tight. "You're the best. Thank you."

"You're welcome."

"Okay, now that the gifts are over, where's the man?" Growing serious, she glanced around the room, obviously looking for Dylan.

"He's in L.A. Or should I say on his way back to L.A."

Nicole frowned. "That snake. I thought you had more time together."

"Something came up."

"You seem okay with it?" Nicole tipped her head to the side, questioning.

"It's not like I have a choice. Look, he lives in L.A. His career is there. His life is there. Mine is here. It's not like we could make a relationship work anyway. Assuming he even wanted something serious."

"Does he?"

"I don't know."

"Do you?"

Holly stood and arranged the blanket over one end of the couch. The colors complemented the room beautifully, and she smiled. "This is gorgeous."

"And you're avoiding my question."

Holly laughed. "That's my prerogative, isn't it?"

Nicole rolled her eyes. "You're going to have to figure things out eventually or you'll make yourself crazy. I need to get going." She rose and started for the door, and Holly followed. "What are you doing for dinner?"

"No real Christmas plans. Want to come back here and we'll have girls' night?"

"Now, that's the best offer I've had in a long time." Nicole hugged her tight. "What about this afternoon?"

"I need to see John."

Nicole sighed in understanding. "I don't envy you."

"I owe him answers." And she owed herself a lot more.

It was time to face her fears once and for all.

* * *

Later that day, Holly drove to John's and knocked on his door.

He greeted her warmly, looked into her eyes and said, "Why do I have the distinct feeling you aren't here with the news I was hoping for?"

She studied him with a fresh, new perspective. His gorgeous green gaze and handsome face would have a smarter woman than her swooning. God, she wished she were smarter because then her life would be so much less complicated.

"Can we talk?" she asked.

He gestured inside with a sweep of his arm, and once they were seated on the leather couch in his spacious den, Holly mustered her courage. "You're such a good man," she said softly.

"But you don't love me."

She shook her head. "Not the way you deserve." And the signs had been there all along. She had never given to him physically or emotionally the way she gave herself to Dylan. Oh, she had tried hard to convince herself she could love John, but the truth is she didn't. She couldn't.

She loved Dylan, and no other man would do. "I'm just so sorry it took me so long to—"

"Don't say you're sorry." He cut her off. "I'm not sorry for the time we had, and I know I learned a lot about myself. Especially about my patience level. It's too damn high," he said with a self-deprecating laugh.

Holly laughed with him before covering his hand with hers. "There's something you need to know though. While we were together I never consciously thought we couldn't have a future because of Dylan."

"I knew that or else I would have given you an ultimatum much sooner. I take it you two are back together?"

"I don't know what we are." She grimaced, unsure how to explain. "He went back to L.A.," she said, deciding that since he was asking, she'd talk to John. Old habits, she mused. They *had* been close, and she'd always confided in him.

"I caught the morning's news," he said, the implication clear.

Besides, Holly knew they watched the same channel. "Interesting stuff, huh?" She ducked her head in embarrassment.

"Is it true?" John touched her shoulder, forcing her to look up, then pinned her with his steady gaze.

"No." She shook her head. "No, it's not."

"You trust Dylan enough to say that with such certainty?"

She nodded, no hesitation in her heart.

"Then why are you in such a bad mood?" John leaned back against the couch, relaxing as they talked like old friends.

Which they were, she thought, feeling more settled than she had in a while. And he was right. She was in an awful mood.

"It sounds like you two finally have everything going for you, no?"

"Yes. No. I don't know. He lives in L.A. Not only is it across the country, but his lifestyle, the people in it, they're Hollywood. I'm small town. What kind of chance do we have?" she asked, expressing all of her doubts and fears.

Not all, a tiny voice in her head chided her.

"Listen to me," John said. "You have exactly the kind of chance that you *want*. If you're looking for excuses to bail on Dylan, I know you can be the master of avoidance. But if you want a future, you're going to have to trust him."

"I do!" She narrowed her gaze. "Didn't I just finish telling you I was certain the gossip about Melanie isn't true?"

"And that's a start. It's just not everything. When's he due back?"

She shrugged. "He didn't say. He just promised he'd return."

"Then I guess it's up to you whether you believe him or you're going to let one mistake the guy made ten years ago ruin any future you two *could* have." In that one sentence, John nailed Holly's last remaining fear.

That Dylan would up and leave her again the way he had before. The last time, he didn't know what he was running to. He had only the idea of fame and fortune beckoning to him. Now, ten years later, he knew what kind of lifestyle awaited him in Hollywood. He was America's favorite movie star.

For how long would he be content with his hometown girl?

She blinked, her eyes burning. "When did you get to be so wise?" she asked John.

"About the time I realized we were over." His lips pulled into a thin tight line.

She had to bite the inside of her cheek to keep from apologizing again. "What about you?" She asked. "Are you going to be okay?"

He nodded with certainty. "I definitely saw this coming. I've been thinking about moving to Boston," he said, surprising her.

"Really?"

"Yep. There's more of a social life there, and since I do want to settle down with the right person, I need more exposure."

"I think the women in the city had better watch out," she said, laughing.

He winked at her, assuring her that he really was going to be just fine.

Would she? Her heart caught in her chest because she realized she *would* miss him as her friend. "I admire you for making the decision and going after what you want in life."

He brushed a kiss on her cheek. "I'd like to be able to say the same thing about you. Think about what I just said, Holly."

She forced a smile. "I will."

In the coming days, with Dylan gone, she'd have plenty of time to focus on her life and make a decision about whether she was ready to put her heart on the line again. Or whether she could live with herself if she chose not to even try.

* * *

Three days passed in which Holly kept busy. She saw patients and readied the office for her new partner. She'd been using the extra room for personal storage, and she needed to clear her things out before the first of the year, when Dr. Tollgate started working. After tackling the boxes and moving them into her own office, she began dusting the bookshelves and desk. She found that keeping busy also helped her think. Office cleaning was akin to clearing her mind and facing what she needed and wanted out of life. What she wanted from Dylan.

He had called her two or three times a day since he'd been gone, testament to his desire to prove he'd changed. That he wasn't leaving her behind—if not without a thought, then without another word for ten years. She didn't know what more he had in mind for them, but she understood that she had to come to terms with her own feelings before he returned.

She shook her head. Her feelings weren't the issue. She loved Dylan. The problem lay with her insecurity. John had called her on it, and she knew he was right.

The door chimes startled her. Wondering if there was an emergency, she headed for the outer room to see who was there. She opened the door, looked around but saw no one. She was about to go back inside when she glanced down. A large manila envelope sat at her door. Inside was a map, a set of directions to what appeared to be someplace about half an hour outside of town and a note. In Dylan's handwriting.

Heart pounding, she stepped back into the office so she could read the letter to herself aloud. "I promised I'd be back, and here I am." She licked her dry lips before continuing. "I can't change the past, but I hope to alter the future. Stop running and meet me. If you dare."

If she dared. She shook her head, laughing and trembling at the same time. Leave it to Dylan to challenge her in the most basic way.

It was simple really. Either she trusted or she didn't. Melanie's fake announcement and her own reaction to it had proven to Holly that she believed in him. Now it was time to question whether she trusted *herself*.

Before now she'd never have pegged herself as an insecure person. Yet she was forced to admit that when it came to men and relationships, she was a complete weenie, and those insecurities dated back to Dylan's departure ten years ago. After he left, she had thrown herself into her studies. Once she'd recovered and started dating again, she'd chosen safe men, none of whom affected her emotions and none of whom gave her that sexual zing she felt with Dylan. They were all good, decent men but posed no threat to her heart.

But now Dylan was back, and he was definitely a threat, not just to the heart she'd taken such good care of, but to everything she'd become as a person. She'd always considered herself confident and capable; after all, she was a doctor who'd been making decisions about her patients for years. What about herself and choices on her own behalf?

She glanced down at the note in her shaking hands. *Stop running and meet me. If you dare.*

Did she dare? She could easily offer Dylan North her heart and maybe even trust in his promise to handle both it and her with care. But was she secure enough in herself to believe she could hold on to him this time?

There it was, her biggest fear exposed.

She could run and never know the happiness she felt certain Dylan could provide, or she could shut the door on the past forever and believe in herself at last. Holly closed the extra office door, and aware of the symbolism, she locked it up tight.

Then she straightened her shoulders, decision made. Damn straight she was secure enough to handle Dylan now. If not, she wasn't the person she thought she was.

And she'd worked too hard and come too far not to believe in the woman Dr. Holly Evans had become.

* * *

Snow covered the ground and big flakes began to fall. The longer Dylan stood on the property he'd own as soon as the legalities had been finalized, the more time he had to convince himself that Holly wouldn't show.

He trusted Nicole to deliver the directions, so he didn't think that was the problem. No, if anything, Holly was still unsure whether she could believe in him again. He'd done everything in his power to convince her. The decision was hers to make.

He rubbed his hands together and shoved them into his jacket pocket. Closing his eyes, he envisioned the house he wanted to build on this land. The only thing was that when he pictured a wife to come home to, it was Holly he saw there. Their children playing in the yard.

In his heart he knew she shared those dreams, and he couldn't make himself believe she'd let *them* down.

"Hi, Dylan."

At first he thought he was imagining the sound of her soft voice until he opened his eyes. She stood before him bundled in a puffy down jacket, scarf and a hat with a small brim. Her eyes were wide and curious.

He was just damn glad to see her. "Hey, babe. Merry Christmas."

She smiled before she shocked him big-time by throwing herself into his arms. Dylan wasn't stupid, and he held on tight. "I missed you," he whispered in her ear.

"I missed you too." She stepped back and studied his face. "Where are we?"

This was it, he thought. The beginning or the end. "It's home." He gestured around the wide expanse of land. "Five acres of grass and trees. Of course, it needs a house and some other necessary things, like a dog and a few kids."

He tried to shoot her a cocky grin but failed. Everything he wanted out of life was on the line, and for the first time, his charm, looks and fame couldn't give it to him.

Only she could.

A dog? Kids? "Home?" Holly asked, stunned.

She blinked and glanced around. The land looked the same as much of the landscape she'd passed while driving out here. A beautiful white landscape covered in snow and ice while the sun shone overhead.

"I own it, or I will once the contract is signed. Actually—" He paused, obviously uncomfortable.

Her heart thudded so loud she was surprised he couldn't hear. He'd bought land here?

"Actually what?" Her voice cracked, she was so afraid of what came next. It was ridiculous being afraid of happiness, but it had been so long since she'd dared to hope or dream.

"Actually, I want us to own it. You and me." He grabbed on to her hands and held them in front of her. "I want to live here and raise our kids here."

"What about L.A.? Your life? Your career?"

He smiled, but it didn't reach his eyes. "I've thought this through, you know. This wasn't an impulse buy. I want you to take some time off and come with me to L.A., so you can see my life and friends for yourself. I want you to be a part of everything that I do."

She swallowed hard, daring to believe. Meeting him here had been the first step. Now she listened with an open heart as well as an open mind. "Go on."

"Then we come back here to live. I'll leave only for movie shoots and, honest to God, I'd planned on cutting back. Doing only what appeals to me creatively because financially I'm already set for life. I'll be here with you as often as I can, and you'll come to me when you can take the time. *We* can make this work. You just need to believe."

Tears dripped down her cheeks, practically turning to ice before they fell. She grasped his face in her hands and looked into his gorgeous blue eyes.

"You have no idea what your leaving the first time did to me. I withdrew, Dylan. I didn't get involved with another man who I thought could hurt me the way you did."

A muscle ticked in his jaw as he listened and replied. "I'm not sure I like where this is headed."

"Shh." She placed her finger over his lips. "You need to hear this as much as I need to say it."

He nodded slowly.

"But I also realize now that there isn't another man who could hurt me that way because there's no one I could ever love the way I love you."

He sucked in a deep breath, and when he released it, a puff of white hovered in the air. "I love you too. I never stopped, not even after I left."

"I know that now."

He brushed at her tears. "We were so young, and I was so stupid."

She shook her head. "We needed to follow the paths we did. It made us who we are."

"And who are we?" he asked.

"Two people who found their way back to each other." She laughed. "Or rather, you found me again. Either way I'm not stupid enough to turn you away." She pulled him into a long, deep kiss, savoring the warmth of his mouth and how he devoured her, as if he could never get enough.

She knew she'd never get enough of him.

Too soon, he pulled back. "You realize there'll be times I'm gone for weeks, maybe months at a time?"

She nodded.

"And you need to trust that while I'm gone, I'm still with you in here." He patted the place above his heart. "You have to know I'll be back, and you need to remember there's no one else but you." His deep gaze never left hers. "No matter what you see, hear or read. Can you do that?"

She nodded again. "Dylan, I love you. It's always been you. And not only do I trust you with my heart, I trust you to remind me not to be an idiot if those old insecurities ever arise." Because she was only human and understood she couldn't promise not to be.

Dylan met her gaze, and in her eyes, he saw everything he was, everything he desired and everything he wanted to be. "Babe, I can do that. I can do anything as long as I have you. And that angel I gave back to you? It was because I want it to top *our* tree. Because you're my Midnight Angel."

She grinned and planted a kiss on his lips. One that was warm, hot, giving and went on and on and on….

EPILOGUE

New England Express

Daily Dirt Column

(Taken from *Entertainment Weekly*) Hollywood heartthrob Dylan North tied the knot on New Year's Day, but not with his former flame, Melanie Masterson, as previously reported. Ms. Masterson was secluded on an island retreat while Dylan North wed hometown girl and first love, Dr. Holly Evans. The two pulled off the coup of the new year, marrying in a private ceremony at a small catering hall called Whipporwill's in Acton, Massachusetts. As of now, details are sketchy, but this reporter was promised an exclusive, complete with wedding photographs of the bride and groom after they return from their honeymoon. One guest who couldn't contain her excitement reported that the desserts were all topped with Marshmallow Fluff.

Stay tuned as more information becomes available.

Thank you for reading MIDNIGHT ANGEL. Don't forget to read the rest of the "Love Unexpected" books:

Solitary Man

Perfect Partners

The Right Choice

If you enjoyed, please tell other readers why you liked this book by reviewing it at your favorite online retailer, as well as Goodreads!

Connect with me online:

If you would like to know when my next book is available, you can:

Visit my website:
www.carlyphillips.com

Sign up for my newsletter:
http://www.carlyphillips.com/newsletter-sign-up/

Follow me on Twitter:
www.twitter.com/carlyphillips

Friend me on Facebook:
www.facebook.com/carlyphillipsfanpage

Follow or Friend me on Goodreads:
http://www.goodreads.com/author/show/10000.Carly_Phillips/

About the Author

N.Y. Times and *USA Today* Bestselling Author Carly Phillips has written over 40 sexy, emotional romance novels. She's a writer, a knitter of sorts, a wife, and a mom to two daughters and two crazy dogs (a Havanese named Brady and a neurotic wheaten terrier named Bailey). She lives in Purchase, NY. Carly is a Twitter and Internet junkie and is always around to interact with her readers.

Anthologies

(http://www.carlyphillips.com/category/books/?series=anthologies)

Truly Madly Deeply (boxed set of Perfect Partners, The Right Choice, Solitary Man)

Sinfully Sweet (also includes The Right Choice and 5 other authors)

More Than Words Volume 7

Santa Baby (Carly's Naughty or Nice novella)

Invitations to Seduction (Carly's Going All the Way – not in print)

Midnight Angel – A "Love Unexpected" Novella

First love and second chances. High school sweethearts, Dylan North and Holly Evans believed their future together was a done deal. But right after graduation, Dylan took off, leaving nothing behind except a hastily written note and Holly's broken heart. Ten years later, Dr. Holly Evans has a great career and a fulfilling life. The last thing she needs is Dylan's visit stirring up old feelings. Especially when she knows the Hollywood superstar can't possibly want to stay. Dylan might have everything money can buy but his life is empty without Holly. Can his unexpected return reignite their love … or does happily ever after only happen in the movies?

Solitary Man – A "Love Unexpected" Novel

When tough Boston cop Kevin Manning promised to care for his fatally wounded partner's family, an unexpected one night stand with the man's grieving sister wasn't part of the plan. No matter how intense the night had been, a woman like Nikki Welles deserves much more than a broken man like Kevin can give, and he leaves the next day. When he returns months later, he discovers everything has changed. Nikki can't regret the baby she's now carrying but she can't forgive Kevin for abandoning her either. Will their unexpected baby teach Kevin he's worthy of love and bring these two unlikely lovers together?

The Right Choice – A "Love Unexpected" Novel

Carly Wexler makes her living as an advice columnist, never realizing she needs a reality check of her own. Convinced that happiness lies along the route she's carefully mapped out for herself, she's been missing living life to its fullest. When her fiance's globe-traveling, photo-journalist brother arrives in time for the wedding, the unexpected punch of desire sends her reeling, forcing her to reevaluate her best-laid plans. Will Carly open her mind as well as her heart and accept that her unexpected love for Mike is the right choice for her after all?

Perfect Partners – A "Love Unexpected" Novel

No sooner had lawyers Chelsie Russell and Griffin Stuart lost their siblings in a car crash than they find themselves fighting for custody of their two year old niece. Griff wins only to discover Chelsie is the only one who can sooth the child's night terrors and fears. Chelsie and Griff bond over the little girl and their growing sexual desire is mutual. But Chelsie's been hurt before and Griff isn't sure he can trust the woman who once tried to take his niece away. What will it take for these two unexpected lovers to believe they can be perfect partners after all?

Made in the USA
Lexington, KY
03 July 2014